MOTHER
EARTH

Picture books by
Nancy Luenn and Neil Waldman

Nessa's Fish
Mother Earth

MOTHER EARTH

By Nancy Luenn
Illustrated by Neil Waldman

ALADDIN PAPERBACKS

First Aladdin Paperbacks edition 1995
Text copyright © 1992 by Nancy Luenn

Illustrations copyright © 1992 by Neil Waldman

Aladdin Paperbacks
An imprint of Simon & Schuster
Children's Publishing Division
1230 Avenue of the Americas
New York, NY 10020

The Library of Congress has cataloged the hardcover edition as follows:

Luenn, Nancy.
Mother earth / by Nancy Luenn; illustrated by Neil Waldman.
p.   cm.
Summary: Describes the gifts that the earth gives to us and the
gifts that we can give back to her.
ISBN 0-689-31668-2
[1. Earth—Fiction. 2. Environmental protection—Fiction.]
I. Waldman, Neil, ill. II. Title.
PZ7.L9766Mo 1992
[E]—dc20   90-19134
ISBN 0-689-80164-5 (Aladdin pbk.)

To all of Earth's children

N.L.

For Davor Bakovic,
whose sensitive readings of this manuscript helped redirect my focus
and ultimately reshaped the paintings found herein

N.W.

The earth is our mother

The ground is her skin

Mountains her bones

Trees and plants her living hair

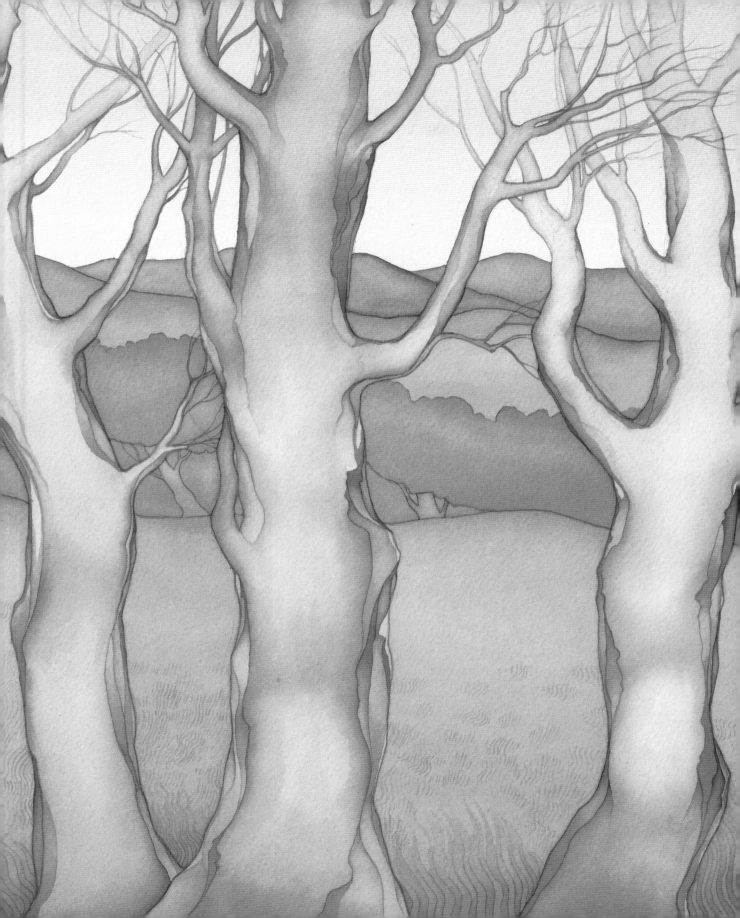

Birds are her songs

And the listening stones her ears

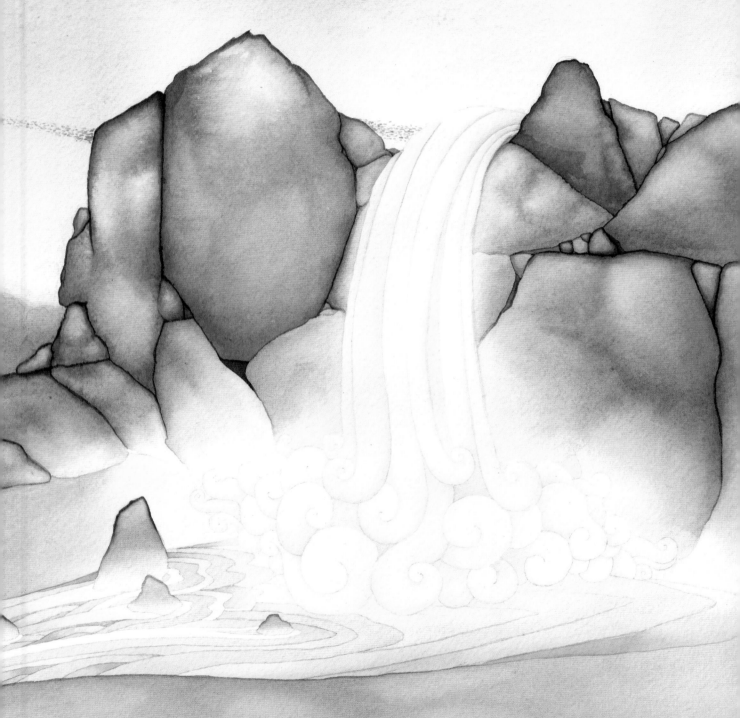

Animals her fingers

Frogs and snakes are her sense of smell
Insects her thoughts

Her dreams the sea and all its swimmers

Water her blood

The air her breath

Sunlight and fire the warmth of her body

We are her eyes

And we are her children

She gives all she is
We take what we can

But what can we give to our mother?

Make her a blanket of leaves
and grass to cover her skin

Plant living hair

Feed her songs
And shelter her fingers

Sit and listen as the stones do

Clear the trouble from her dreams

And fill the streams with swift young fish

To use her gifts well

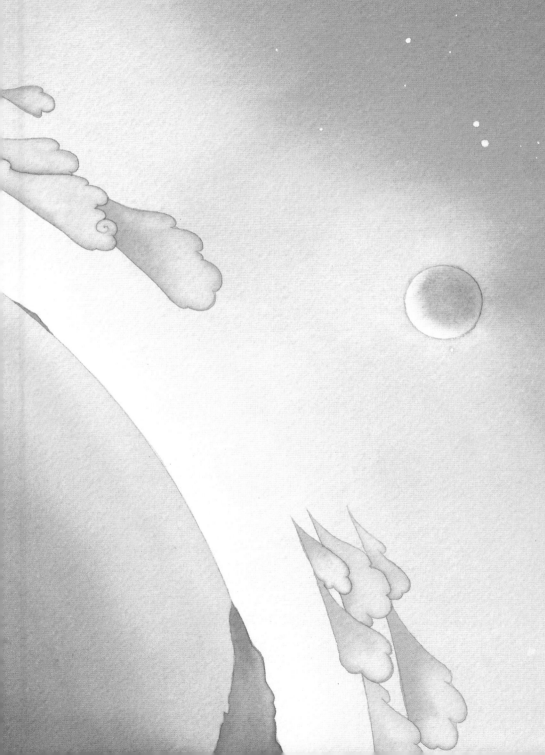

And give back what we can

This is a gift that we give to our mother Earth

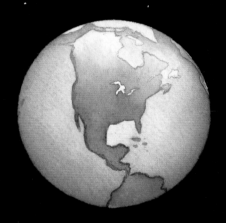